Staying is Nowhere

Staying is Nowhere

by

Ann B. Knox

SCOP Publications, Inc.
College Park, Maryland

Writer's Center Editions
Bethesda, Maryland

1996

STAYING IS NOWHERE
Copyright © 1996 by Ann B. Knox

These poems or earlier versions of them appeared in the following periodicals and anthologies: *Apalachee Quarterly*: "Quinsy"; *Blue Guitar*: "Readying"; *Cumberland Poetry Review*: "Begin," "Biker's Girl", "Preparing to Go"; *Fine Comb*: "London Bridge"; *Green Mountains Review*: "Go for the Root," "The Understood You," "Staying Is Nowhere"; *Hungry as We Are*: "The First Time"; *Monocacy Valley Review*: "Photographs of my Mother"; *Negative Capability*: "I Dream Old Dylan Came Back"; *New York Quarterly*: "I Divorce You"; *Ohio Poetry Review*: "Clematis," "The Space Between Us"; *Out of Season, an Anthology*: "In Memoriam"; *Passager*: "The First Time"; *Plum Review*: "A Friend Leaves"; *Poet's Market*: "She Remembers her Husband"; *Poets On*: "In Memoriam," "To Part"; *Potomac Review*: "Peat Bog"; *Sisters, an Anthology*, Still Waters Press: "She Learned of Glaciers"; *Warren Wilson Review*: "Glacier Bay," "Woman who Paints Dogs"; *WPFW: 89.3 FM, an anthology*: "A Boy Brings his Grandmother a Stone Bird." These poems first appeared in *Poetry* and are copyright by the Modern Poetry Association: "Bereave" in 1994, "Circles" in 1992, and "The Boy Brings his Grandmother a Stone Bird" in 1991.

I am grateful to the Pennsylvania Council on the Arts for fellowships which helped support me while writing these poems, and to the Atlantic Center for the Arts and the Virginia Center for the Creative Arts for unbroken time to work in a quiet place during several residencies.

I wish to thank Jean Johnson for her help in editing this manuscript, and Maxine Combs, Elizabeth Follin-Jones and Elisavietta Ritchie for their support, encouragement and thoughtful critiques in the course of creating these poems.

Photographs by Thomas Ligamari
Cover design by Jeanne Krohn

ISBN 0-930526-19-8
Library of Congress Catalog Card No. 95-071843

SCOP Twenty-one in a Series
First Edition
Printed in the United States of America

SCOP Publications, Inc.	Writer's Center Editions
Box 376	4508 Walsh Street
College Park, MD 20740	Bethesda, MD 20815

for Ann Fraser Brewer

CONTENTS

PREPARING TO GO
Preparing to Go • 3
Circles • 4
Among Low Hills • 5
I Thank My Sister • 6
I Learn of Glaciers • 7
The Understood *You* • 8
Photographs of My Mother • 10
Story About Jim • 11
Toad • 12
Readying • 13
The First Time • 14
Clematis • 15
To Part • 16
I Divorce You • 18
She Remembers her Husband • 19
I Dream Old Dylan Came Back • 20
A Friend Leaves • 21
Begin • 22

POEMS FOR JOANNA
Dream of My Daughter • 25
Bereave • 26
Holding Joanna • 27
The Next Day • 28
In Memoriam • 29

NOTHING SIMPLE
Small Things • 33
To Get Lost • 34
What's Happening? • 35

London Bridge is Falling • 36
Peat Bog • 37
Entering Siena • 38
Woman Who Paints Dogs • 39
Go for the Root • 40
Hedge • 41
Quinsy • 43
Inertia • 44
Nothing New to See • 45
Losing Sight • 46
After Cataract Surgery • 47
Pawpaw • 48

STAYING IS NOWHERE
Etymology of *Journey* • *51*
Trying Out a Blazer 4-By • 52
Bozeman, Montana • 53
With My Sister at Glacier Bay • 54
Biker's Girl • 55
Thanks to Cavafy • 56
Where I've Been • 57
The Space Between Us • 58
Approaching the Crone • 59
She Folds Her Arms • 60
A Boy Brings His Grandmother a Stone Bird • 61
Staying Is Nowhere • 62

Preparing to Go

PREPARING TO GO

I'm an old hand at journeys, making ready,
closing accounts, collecting passports,
Fodors, diversions for the voyage. I'm used to
stiff partings, difficult goodbyes.

Those travels were meant — a new posting,
visit to parents, holidays with the children,
but this time nothing is required. I have no map
or guidebook, no ticket and no particular reason
to go. This house is satisfactory but as days draw in,
a sudden smoke of starlings startles unease.

I stroke the stone bird on the table beside me,
sun catches a gold-framed painting — a woman
in a red shawl watching from a window the street
below — people, traffic, a vendor selling fruit.

Now I am expected nowhere and without luggage,
both hands free I leave to enter a new
country unframed, unglassed where passers-by
pay no heed and I recognize no one.

A crone offers an apple but refuses my coin.
The fruit, she says, *is already paid for.*
The smell of autumn rises like light around me,
I pull my red shawl close against the wind, it seems
all other journeys have been practice for this.

CIRCLES

It is dangerous to break a round thing,
to disturb a circle. The foot must center
neat on a man-hole lid, the yellow crayon
keep within the sun. When my brother peeled
a golfball and unwound the mile-long
rubber twine, he stopped before its center,
the poison core that gives the power to bound.

A life-saver grows thin as an old wedding-
ring and shatters to curved needles on the tongue.
It is dangerous to break a round thing,
but I disturbed the circle, burst out, wanting
something wild, something risky and I lied.

Our beers sweat rings on the table, the candle
throws a round of yellow light, you speak
of the children, of plans, until I reach out
to draw a line between us. My finger slices
a wet circle, crosses the curved edge
of flickering light. You trace a coaster rim
but do not look at me, knowing it is dangerous
to break a round thing, to disturb a circle.

AMONG LOW HILLS

Here, among low hills
where land gives way to sea
I first learned the words
spindrift, *wetland*, *ebb*.

Twice daily the river spread
flat and blue filtering
through marsh-grass, holding
in balance earth and sky

but always the river turned
and pulled back to a narrow cut
exposing mudflats slick as offal,
the surface troubled by slithers

and the suck of a branched tree
that grooved the mud with twisted
order as the peat-dark
stream funneled down to the sea.

I watched chaos create
its own patterns, a northeaster
combed the willow straight
and tossed a neap tide

over the seawall salting
the well, I learned sky
was a universe curving
back on itself forever

and imagined infinity ended
in barnacled gray granite
that lasted for a single beat
before a seam rent the wall

to further sky. I still
wonder what matrix holds
the whole — space, ether,
the clear jelly of spawn.

I THANK MY SISTER

You taught me that mare's tails at evening
meant rain, that "I" alone is always a capital,
that our mother had to come back and you warned me
to watch for a sudden widening of her eyes.

When we claimed a hollow tree behind the sumacs
you knew we needed a low and secret entry,
you knew of dangers I had not imagined:
nettles, quick-sand, underground anger.

When cloud-shadows crossed the marsh, you said,
Run, stay with the light, but we were
overtaken. How did you learn without someone
to show you, someone to point the way?

After you left she bought me an elegant dress
I hated but when I wore it, she frowned. I tried
to be safe, to read signs, do what was wanted,
but it was not satisfactory and you were away, married
living in your own house, learning new signs.

I LEARN OF GLACIERS

The week we studied glaciers, the land's form
changed, the low round hills beyond
my attic window acquired history and a name,
drumlin. Snow centuries-deep pressed
denser than ice, spread over borders,
mountains, grid-marks, to arrive at this place.

I was grateful for reasons — to know that warm
blew in and milk-blue melt left valleys
scoured and lined with river-sorted drift,
that claw marks on granite were ice-claws,
I loved the evidence of what earth did to itself.

Danger lay not in ice, but downstairs
where people moved from room to room, went
away and came back or didn't come back, they told
stories, then claimed they weren't true. *Where
was Gretl's father?* No rule held, no
certain gravity or law of frost and heave,
only my own ordering gave uneasy shape
to a landscape without reason, without melt.

THE UNDERSTOOD *YOU*

At eight I could not grasp
who was addressed when I called,
> *Help, save me.*

An imperative, they said, a nameless
you. Father, mother, God, perhaps.

Later I whispered,
> *Take me. Hold me.*

I trusted the hand I held,
loved its rifts, mounds
and raised blue veins, but
when palm slid from palm,
who did I mean when I cried,
> *Don't let go?*

The words melted as fog
on autumn mornings,
I tried again, this time,
> *Come back.*

But only cicada song rose
from the oak. No one came.

I am accustomed now to silence
but still imagine help at hand.
Reeds clog the pasture pond,
a whine of insects
holds over stagnant water,
I pick a leech from my arm.
> *Take me from this place.*

Feet slip on the clay bank,
I grab a root and pull
to an outcrop where the valley
opens whole — a farmer plowing,
the distant highway's metallic flow,
mountains beyond.

A new imperative gathers,
this time I understand
the silent you
is me, the words
instructions to myself,
    Move on. Move on.

PHOTOGRAPHS OF MY MOTHER

You wear a white dress, a white bow
in your hair and you hug your sister, posed
surely by the man under the black cloth.
Your smile has held too long, the bow has slipped.

In this you're thirteen, dressed in a linen smock,
your brows dark, a single braid down your back,
arms holding each other. You look away
as if fixing this image was of no moment.

And here in fierce dry country, you stand
on the canyon's rim, back to the camera,
one high-laced boot rests on a boulder
your head turns as if a sound jarred the silence.

These were taken before I knew you, yet
you are no stranger. I recognize the smile
meant to pacify, the distance between the body
unaccustomed to itself and desire for ease,

and how, for a startled moment on the cliff's rim
you meet emptiness — no one to judge,
no one to please — and alert for a pebble loosed
or movement among the rocks, you are wholly there.

STORY ABOUT JIM

    (For my brother, Mike)

I made you promise not to tell, then
told you a lie, a story about a friend.

I was twelve and had never touched a boy but knew
the sour smell of them in school hallways,

how the dry crabs of their hands snatched
a jack-ball or peeled paper from a Milky Way.

Jim I made different, he was smart, nice
and never shamed me. You were nine and believed.

Was he good at sports? I wasn't certain —
a ball lofted over left field, Jim following,

mitt ready for the neat thwack. After the game
girls swarmed round him, so I gave us an island.

What we did there was survive. Together we built
a driftwood hut, Jim fished, I walked the tideline

collecting washed up bottles, shells, rope.
Odd I made him so ordinary, almost like me,

but we each invent our Fridays, our cellmates —
parrot, cockroach, rat. I needed someone

to believe I was alive, even a lie of being alive
and you did, all your life. At the end

you said you'd never told about the island
or Jim, not anyone, ever. And I had forgotten

how fifty years ago I imagined the ocean quiet,
small waves fanning the sand, the sea-wrack

rich with treasure and someone watching.
It wasn't Jim, but you, Mike, who knew I was there.

TOAD

Burdock grows rank behind the barn, gnats
thicken the air where a shadow of hog-killing

lingers after decades. Wading the sunless path
through thigh-high weeds, something stirs at my feet.

I squat. A toad hunkers low to the ground,
brown, warty, with eyes reflecting trapezoids of sky

and three blunt fingers spread like the butcher
who unabashed leans stubs against the counter.

Without stir or shift of eye, the toad flicks
its tongue and a green wing angles from its mouth,

a jaunty cigarette, and like the eighth grade clown,
the toad swallows, wing disappears in a half-smile.

Jimmy Sandro did that, he made us laugh
and he challenged nice Miss Gwynn. She pretended

he wasn't there, but he was — always a rustle
around him, wind, a seethe in the current.

Once Jimmy touched me — on my wrist, his hand
light, fingerbacks dusky with brown hair —

and a strange heat rose from my belly. I knew
this was danger and the danger was in me.

Why do I think of Jimmy now? He worked
for his father, wrapped meat in butcher paper,

a loop of string, knots easily undone.
I wonder where he went — his smile, his quick

hands. Strange to recall the stir of him
here on the cold north side of the barn.

READYING

A girl watches her mother
prepare: silk slip,
long dress, hair
covered with a blue net.

The mirror reflects a careful
line of red, her mother
bending toward herself
intent, close as an enemy.

The girl knows this readying
matters, but for what wondrous
event, what satisfaction,
she can not yet imagine.

FIRST TIME

He took her hand and drew it down
to a heat-nest of hair, to a column
base, her belly recoiled, but her hand,
obedient, lightly tried the surface.
Smooth it was, resilient, alive.

Once in Mr. Haskell's boat an eel
had spiraled up her arm, a green coil
thick as rope and slick, the muscle of it
pressing her muscle, its small sloped eye
malevolent. Where was her fear born?

She recalled boys practicing taunt and swagger,
an image of thick fingers on the window-sill,
her leaps across the cave beneath her bed
and viney dreams of fruit-heavy branches
where something hidden troubled the leaves.

Later when melon sweetness laced the air,
her breasts stirred to a touch and with a sudden
loosening, layers fell away as pleasure slid over
the brim of fear and her body opened to astonishment.

CLEMATIS

We do not touch to say goodbye. You carry
an armful of books to the car and come back
for your duffle. Air stirs as you pass,
you do not look at me but old habits of discourse
stay, small courtesies — I proffer coffee,
you comment on the pink clematis by the door
that blooms this year for the first time.
These exchanges cannot camouflage a parting.

I watch for some sign, a gesture of your hand,
a bend toward as we speak of the children, car,
mail to be forwarded. I want to forgive you,
forgive myself, be forgiven. Without looking back
you brush the vine, a few petals scatter
as if your going were a simple matter.

TO PART:

>(etymology from Partridge's Origins)

No wonder *to part* stirs
unease. *To make ready,
as to beget children.*
Month after emptying month,
spring into summer and at last
a full fall. (See *parent,
prepare, poor.*)

In Hittite, *to break,
divide*, as we
broke a loaf among us
you, me, the children,
you cut cheese as I combed
strands of our daughter's hair.

In Celtic, *a thigh, a leg*,
(ah yes, that parting.)
In Sanskrit, *reward*
and there were many — waking
with you beside me, hikes
across the downs, a cafe
by the harbor's edge — oysters,
cold wine — good moments
when we knew and were glad.

*Part of a whole, a shared
wall* — something
incomplete alone and yet
a barrier like silence
or a book held *to separate
oneself from*, or perhaps
only to catch the light.

Particle or wave? It's we
the observers who determine what
to see, what messages to read.
Odd, after all the years
away, it's you I think of
when I address the word, *part*.

I DIVORCE YOU

It's simple. Say it three times
in the presence of witnesses, if
their presence troubles, practice
on the porch, say it aloud to the hawk,
whisper it in the round holes of carpenter bees,
press your lips against the pine's bark,
say it and breathe the smell of resin, say it
to the hand you hold over your mouth,
say it to the mirror, note your eyes
and teach them to repeat the words.

When you have it perfectly, knock
on the library door and walk in. He'll
turn but you won't see his face for the light
behind him, only the way his hand holds
open the book, how age has thickened his knuckles,
how his body leans toward you hunched like a target.
The words crouch ready in your throat, but remember,
once they are sprung, you can count on nothing.

SHE REMEMBERS HER HUSBAND

Two crows hunt the meadow
moving in small starts, one
halts, feet wide, the other
crouched, opens its beak
ready for the quick strike,
the head's toss. No sign
passes between them, but together
they turn, unfold ragged wings
and skim over the sumacs
close as fighter planes.

I DREAM OLD DYLAN CAME BACK

He scratched at the kitchen door,
clicked across the tiles with his low-
slung swag. I squatted to circle his neck,
feel his body curve in welcome — same
red collar, same lop-ear shriveled
from a fight. Remember, we bathed it,
hands touching over the open wound.

Where have you been? It's ten years since
we buried you in the meadow, there's
a hollow where the mower leaves grass
ragged and berries invade the stubble.

Must I rearrange my life now, set out
your waterbowl, your scrap of carpet?
Do you come back to remind me I've been
too long without this rise of gladness,
that welcome lay too long unused?

But you'll leave again. Besides, I have
grown accustomed to my own order — books,
the hard blue hills. I'm glad you came,
I miss you, but don't stay, don't stay.

A FRIEND LEAVES

We walk the pond's edge
and you tell me the letter has come.
I'm glad for you, glad
the months of waiting are over.
Your voice reaches past
the mossed bank, past this valley.

The pond water is dark,
last year's leaves tile the bottom
and a smoke of green weed wavers
in a slight current, spawn
hangs like a shimmering brain.

I have been here before, watched
a son disappear into summer, a lover
merge with distant traffic
and a neighbor drive to a new life,
van riding low, children waving
silence folding behind
and everything thinking.

BEGIN

Sit, write one word
short and clean, some
thing you can touch—
ash, leaf, dog.

> Ash in the mayonnaise lid
> smells of oil when he
> twists out a stub,
> scoring another dark
> bull's eye.

> Under the radiator a leaf
> from the rose geranium
> curls and shrivels,
> a miniature monkey's paw—
> three wishes is it?
> Be careful.

> The dog is old, don't
> count on him, he'll go
> as others have — a sudden
> swerve and thunk, oddly
> no blood, or you call
> and call through empty woods,
> listen at night
> for clicks across the porch
> for the lap-lap, lap-lap.

Are you sure you want
to start this, another
beginning, another long wait?

Poems for Joanna

DREAM OF MY DAUGHTER

I was washing the dishes
when she came into the kitchen
to make tea. She was eight
still, the way I remembered.

Knowing it was a dream, I
pressed back the light
rising like mist from hills.
She poured carefully
as if no one were present,
as if certain of what to do.

She filled a fragile Chinese cup,
pink, green and red it was
with tiny figures — one
played a reed pipe, another
bowed, arms folded in loose sleeves.
She turned the stove flame
low and set the cup upon it.

No, I said, *no. The cup
will break.* I touched,
her thick brown hair,
she looked at me and
like a flute note,
the long sorrow rose
out and out.

BEREAVE: etym. see *rob*

It happened before. This time
we found the door ajar, window
open, a ghost of curtains
blowing in and air still moving
as if someone had gone from the room.

We felt a new absence, noticed
a blank where the bronze whippet stood,
silver candlesticks not there
and in the bedroom, open drawers
flowering with silk scarfs,
the velvet box missing — rings,
brooch, the string of pearls
you gave me after her birth.

We look at each other and say nothing.

We would have passed them on
and much else. What might have been
is taken away and we are left
knowing absence will travel with us —
gaps, small hollows, a hand
held out, no one to take it —
and like risen bread, empty places
become texture and grain,
matrix for all that follows.

HOLDING JOANNA

There is no grace in this still landscape,
no generous ferocity of birth or gentling here
where twisted candles of cypress pierce
white sky, where light corrodes and wire-
thin shadows underlie squat stone.

> I cannot see her face, but her hair slides
> through the brush, a brief brown current
> that curves as a stream curves over a log.
> Her clothes on the floor hold the shape
> of running, and on the wall her drawing —
> a riderless horse, mane flying — stretches
> in wide strides across the empty paper.

Nothing moves on this gradual gray road
edged with dusty mullein, glare flattens
the jut that gives rock-ledges sheer
and boulders substance. My fist holds the sun.
Light cannot free shadow nor stones
claim their mass, no wind breaks the field's
surface, no poppies stain again the wheat until
my hand opens to the pain of losing pain.

THE NEXT DAY

    (For the others)

Afterwards, we took a picnic to a gorge,
a place we'd never been before. It smelled
of moss and wet rock, you built dams,
made villages of twigs and no one quarreled.

An echo edged every sound, every
gesture held sharp as the line between
shade and blinding light, sun on our back
and the cave-cold wind roughing our skin.

We nested bottles among stones in the river
and unpacked the basket watching our hands,
our words, not knowing what to do
with our appetites: bread, plums, chocolate.

I failed to say it then, so I say it now: *Weep,
weep, dance, let your body learn its grief, reach
for the beat below the stillness, listen,
trust your feet to know the moves, your arms*

*the stretch that breaks to an unwalled place
where sudden open stuns the wrapped heart,
where sound lifts as a goldfinch over a field
and fierce joy spills from the taste of plums.*

One forgets pain and the body's in-draw, even
the huge emptiness, what stays are words
unsaid, acts not taken and the ways
we hold the terrible knowing at bay.

IN MEMORIAM

Before you fade
to a dozen sepia stills
and the mist
furring your skin dissolves,
I bring you a lover.
He'll lick swirls in the down
of your back, hold
the plum-firm breasts
you never grew, and lean
over your eyes
as a traveler over a well.

I take your hand
turn your palm
down toward his fingers,
valleys, hills.
As you touch
small moons tug my veins
and I feel a weight,
the gravity of all Earth.

What force it takes
to separate my hands
from that sweet pull.

Nothing Simple

SMALL THINGS

I line on the window sill a fox skull,
compass, stone axehead from a Utah canyon,
beach pebbles, dim now, uninteresting.

Each object fits my palm close as a tight-
fleshed Baldwin apple that grew by the marsh
where I used to walk the tide-line collecting

cork floats, shells, a roil of twine.
My brother found crab-traps, a barrel,
but I passed by what I couldn't carry

and hid my findings, ashamed for choosing
small, for the absence of what mattered. Later
big things accrued — cars, house, family.

I tried to keep them contained, the garden tidy,
but hollyhocks grew wild, children spread
into trees and meadows, waves broke

over the seawall salting the ground.
Though this cabin is spare, I still like
hand-sized things but have learned there's nothing

simple about fissures in a skull, nothing slight
in a tool's curve or compass needle's swing.

TO GET LOST

If you go into the woods to hide expecting
them to find you, they probably will,

but if you want not to be found, become
a wilderness, hold still as a lichened boulder

or let kudzu take you in as it did
the abandoned cabin in the draw. Tendrils

slithered up walls until no one remembered
a house was there — hand-hewn chestnut logs,

cracked windows, green light in an empty room
where cabbage roses peel like continents from a map.

Once you are gone, after a brief wondering,
they become accustomed to your absence and skirt

the vines tenting the hollow. Safe now
to inhabit your secret place, you learn

the floor's tilt, the shadows' daily path,
you befriend the black-snake that goes forth

into daylight and returns shining, warmed by sun.
When voices draw near and pass by —

lovers' low talk, a quarrel — you listen,
not to words, but to your own silent question:

Do I wait for footsteps to approach my door,
for a click of the latch, for someone to come?

WHAT'S HAPPENING?

Wind gusts from the west
laying press on the hay,
a wren holds to a branch,
drops, lifts, accommodating
itself, riding the whip.

A child on a bike,
arms wide, balances,
swerves, rights herself.

We laugh, knowing
the unsteady edge,
the moment before wave
and surfer join, when we shed
will and give over
to curved green water.

LONDON BRIDGE IS FALLING

Earth cools, deep plates click to rest,
the sound of fast water dwindles as hills
slump to swamp, as tundra spreads to the sea.

Fathoms under, Venice settles, gold mosaics
crack, silt fills Torcello's nave and no one
reads the Virgin's kohl-rimmed eyes or the column
of her suffering, her joy, that stay against
gravity which for centuries held and gave heart.

Soft tissue decays, bones go under,
an essence leaves the body — the wit of it,
the will, the power to see a thing not there,
to make in the mind a cello, lighthouse, bridge.

Does this impulse cease that is the sum of us,
the reach — out, toward, across? To what
we do not know, but we know the stretch matters
even fallen stones: Troy, Mycenae, Chaco.

Can we imagine our own going under — tide
flooding the marshes, the daily ebb, elms
streaming in the wind and no one to be grateful?

PEAT BOG

If you want to know
what matters
study the peat-bog,
sphagnum layered
a hundred fathoms deep,
its surface green, smelling
of growth, of rot.

Each cell holds
form and unsprung
heat, each for a season
quickened the fen,
then under press
of its own kind, sank.

The bog will take a sheep
in minutes or a fox
or a man and for centuries
muscle and bone
transform in darkness
to new matter. Above

cells burgeon in the sun,
each pushes toward a given
structure and each,
within frail walls,
carries a separate death.

ENTERING SIENA

I remember entering the ochre city, bars,
flower sellers, curved streets with buildings
full of history, and how the first evening
in a cafe by the fountain, I laid claim

with a surge of recognition as if already acquainted
with the aproned waiter, the amber light.
Pigeons on the basin's rim tilted to drink
as they had for centuries, the quick dip,

the iridescent sheen as I expected. Even
the wine, rough on my tongue, was familiar.
We can know loss, even of what was never
ours, places we only pass through.

I reached to recall how I knew the cobbled streets,
unaware this need to connect with memory's source
would surface again and again, a secret ache
rising suddenly to trouble a late afternoon.

WOMAN WHO PAINTS DOGS

She paints them big — a tongue
wide as an empty sock, fringed lip,
paws waffle-sized with hair thick
as tundra grass between the pads.

The sleeping husky curls into himself,
tail filters the indrawn cold, whiskers
whitened by a brush of deep zero. This is no
arctic monochrome, the dog's coat is streaked
with madder, the V between his eyes dark purple

and he is not still. His forepaws twitch
as if touching a small live thing and the painter
knows the body answers to its own circuitry —
three times round before bedding, the sudden
crouch at movement on the ice or silent run.

She knows the quick halt and swing round
at her whistle are ways learned from her
and these she cannot trust. She remembers
as a young girl how her eyes' shift acknowledged
power but did not erase defiance. Under the icepack
water moves, thermal currents lift and sink.

She imagines dog dreams rising from distant
memory — warm teat, the small close
sounds of litter-mates and below these,
beyond the drive to stay alive, some
unnamed certainty, formless as pure color.

GO FOR THE ROOT

Go for the root, the stem,
the underground white worm
taut with growth that drills

through forest duff as nodes
swell, readying to break out
on bud, leaf and thorn.

Grasp the beginning, the thing
itself before gloss or cumber
diverts its force and draw

from that the power to know.
Be glad as the tongue is glad
to touch old base words —

salt, house, bed, stone —
they recall the bite and sting
of blown seaspray, shelter

and a warm place where the body
curls dreaming of water's
suck, or weigh in your palm

a quartz pebble split from bedrock.
These things are whole
as words that name them and house

an essence as a wineglass
holds within it sound
until a flick frees

a fine note to shimmer
out, or as a root
has power to draw in

elements that feed, burgeon
and transform into a press up
toward light, toward sky.

HEDGE:

> see *haw: hawthorn berry, hence OE hag, haggar (untamed hawk), MHG hecksa* (from ORIGINS, Partridge)

To play safe, I bet
both sides, announce
I am old, a crone,

you can't blame me.
I plant a thornbush fence
to pen myself against

loss by claiming loss —
brothers, lover, child —
those who taught me

to tie a bowline or watch
fog lift from the ridge
and melt to astounding blue.

I use them now as a thicket
to stave off the press
of emptiness, although I know

no hedge will stay disaster.
Yet the mind invents its hexes —
circles, crosses, stars —

designs to soothe itself,
hair rope looped to ward off
snakes, a chalk ring.

To the hawk spiraling
on a rising thermal, our
stonewalls, barbed wire

and boxwood borders become
frail as rings tapped
by gnats on stagnant water.

We old women know this,
but still brew our dark tea
and hand young mothers

a hawthorne root — *Plant this*
for your child's safekeeping.

QUINSY:

> Derives by either contraction or slovening from ML *quinancia*, from Gr *kunankhe*, a dog collar...hence a very sore throat. (from ORIGINS, Partridge)

No wonder this ache, this flushed
face and fever. When I swallow,
a red collar studded with silver
bites against the rising, a choke-
ring tightens on my throat.

I slump among damp pillows
and limp sheets, hair loose
as seaweed, the mind frets
sorry for its slipshod state,
too pitiful to will other.

There's something easeful in giving
over and with this ailment
no blame falls on me.
Sleet clicks on the window,
the dog whimpers and licks my hand.

In spite of throb and restless
turnings, as long as someone
notes this misery, there's pleasure
to be derived from slovening.

INERTIA

To break inertia takes an outside force.
Watch a child toe back the swing then toss
her body out and pull against the rope
to start the narrow arc, the long slope
that counters gravity, a pendulum set loose.

A sled-dog leans against the harness,
slings his weight left then right, his paws
rake ice to free the runners, start the slip
for to break inertia takes an outside force.

A car stalled in the pull of its own mass
or a perched boulder left by retreating ice —
these cannot shift without a change of slope,
without hand or press to move them. What hope
have I to loose the sullen hold of loss,
if to break inertia takes an outside force.

NOTHING NEW TO SEE

I have used up this view, there's nothing
new to see, like a photograph in an album
or memory of somewhere I once was, the scene
is flat, empty, leached of color. I've had

enough long views of stubble fields
and loose gray cloud, give me a stir,
wind from another quarter, sun angled low
to expose the cirque of a fox's earth or scat
laced with fur and fine crushed bone.

I'm free to leave, but to change my site
shifts the whole landscape — borders go,
thresholds, the rim of woods and I can blame
no one for loss of edges that held at bay
the sudden widening, the terrible opening out.

LOSING SIGHT

Through the window I glimpse a blue spruce
on the wood's verge, but when I move
it moves — my sweater reflected in glass.

A hawk perches so long in the oak
I go to the doorway, feathers
shrivel to a cluster of dried leaves.

A tweed coat tossed by the roadside
becomes a dead fox, pelt bloodied,
slit to an outcrop of sun-white ribs

and yesterday, someone crossed the field
slowly, listing a bit on each step,
I recognized your arms' swing

your hands curled as if
holding some frail thing, but
when you turned it was Ellen,

my neighbor, carrying a gift
of brown eggs and a reason
to sit awhile on the steps and talk.

When my sightline curves past
distant hills as light curves
around earth, I know I cannot

stay the perched hawk or own
a remembered stride and I have no
hold on the startling loveliness of bone.

AFTER CATARACT SURGERY

Aware of an ache behind closed lids,
I wake slowly. It is morning but dark
as in a barn, then I remember and hold still.
I allow a crack, an underbrush of lashes
and light knifes in dazzling blue and white —

walls, sheets, the Delft lamp a deep
cobalt I'd not seen before. I lift my head,
the nether eye returns familiar honey
to the room. So this was lost — color,
clean, hard-edged as bleached laundry.

How many shifts has the body made to accommodate
its aging? I fumble for a word, lean to hear
a thrush-call, but what troubles most
are changes hidden, too gradual to note
as the amber world I've grown accustomed to.

I want to know what is, to touch the silk-
dry skin of a black-snake, taste
salt, smell horse sweat or water
tainted by old marigolds and be aware
a yellowed lens has filtered out the blue.

What other censors keep reality at bay —
memory's black pencil, the tongue's forgetting,
a thickened drum or the mind's neat scalpel
that excises secret griefs and shames leaving
the self diminished by what it cannot recognize?

Yet I regret the lost gold light,
the soft glow and innocence of not knowing
the world I saw was altered by my own body.

PAWPAW

We sang of them when we were
six — *picking up pawpaws,*
put 'em in your pocket.
soft-edged I thought them
like a rabbit's foot, later

I imagined weight, a bulge
in an apron pocket, but until
last week, I never saw one.

Walking by the canal, my friend
stopped under a tree, leaves
smooth but limp now in early fall,
she reached to lift out a pale green
globe and dropped it in my palm.

The fruit fit the hollow
neat, the surface firm
but pliant, its curve against
my cheek released a drift,
faint, wild, sweet
as a far-off flute.

My thumbnail broke the skin
to a startle of slick black seeds
buried in translucent flesh
that gave under my teeth, slid
across the tongue spreading light

unknown for six decades. I am glad
this spill of pleasure waited
and welcome a fresh opening,
the old stir loosed again
strange, familiar, new.

Staying is Nowhere

ETYMOLOGY OF *JOURNEY*: *See Diana*

Of course, it begins with the gods —
divine, of the sky, luminous.
The long drawn light of this arctic
afternoon rakes the tundra fells
and wakes on the mind's edge
disquiet and a need to move toward.

*Zeus, Jupiter, keeper of thunderbolts
and stones used in the taking
of an oath.* What hard promise binds me
to move north through barren land?
Something I don't yet know beyond
the open valley, the bare slopes.

And *Jove.* I raise my tin cup, nod
across the campfire to ragged peaks
and slowly drink the thick red wine.

Portugese deos, *becomes in Pidgin,*
joss, *a domestic deity of luck.*
This mossy bank shelters me from wind,
the kindling is dry, cedar-smoke heady
and yesterday the stream gave me a trout.

But dies *occurs disguised in* dismal:
a series of unlucky days — a tire
gone flat, windshield nicked by gravel
thrown from a truck and this morning, fog
closed in, blanking the wide country.

I pressed through a circle of mist, knowing
a journey promises nothing certain
but a day's travel, another chance to let go
expectation, to take in what is — the road,
gods, luck, and now, this late gold light.

TRYING OUT A BLAZER 4-BY

A hundred and sixty-five horses over
a truck chassis — it rides high and the view
opens beyond car-lot fence to fields,
to hills. On the road I'm level with an Exxon tanker,
as we pass the driver lifts a thumb in greeting.

I am unused to the quick response, the surge
uphill, I've settled for what's adequate,
but the sly taste of power meagers that, an appetite
wakes for steeper slopes, rougher tracks.

A bicyclist yaws against the grade, his dog
loping beside him, I gun the motor and they're
a blip in the rearview mirror. Enhanced
by a V-8 engine and the arrogance it bestows,
a hidden penchant to belittle outs and with a rush
of scorn I pull past a white sedan,
the woman driving, gray-haired as I.

Wait, hold on. This is how wars begin.

I downshift and swerve onto a lumber road,
shocks take the washboard bumps, wheels
crush a burst of Christmas fern but a fallen
pine tree blocks my way. I stop, kill
the motor and sudden silence clamps in.

Then rustle, tick, the sharp slice of a jay's
call and a drift of something heady, sweet
I cannot name. Just as well this halt
to turbulence that skewed me from a well-mapped
path. It's not the loosing of horses I fear,
but the unbridled wilderness opened in my belly.

BOZEMAN, MONTANA

The mountain passes were narrow, the grades steep,
now in this valley oats ripen and on the fields'
margins, stand small cities of beehives.

A draft from the place is familiar, a homing draw,
but how many mistakes I have made thinking: *This
is it, here I will be allowed.* I'd call Main Street

mine, load my pickup at the feed-store, my dog
riding the sacks. Ed at Guns & Ammo would blue my rifle,
the checker at Ben Franklin know my name.

Coming from white sun, the Wheel-Inn is dark.
A table of men, ranchers I'd guess, fall
silent watching me. One lights a cigarette.

Had someone a tip on beef sales or is talk
forbidden before a stranger who might find a hold
on this valley that has no room for new-comers?

I unfold a road map to signal: *I am a traveller,
do not concern yourselves.* The waitress pours coffee.
"Where're you headed? Where're you from?"

I name places I have never been. She smiles
and pulls from her apron a cluster of creamers,
her hand wide, as if offering figs to a pilgrim.

My lie is simple, but breaks all liens here.
I want to settle without pretense, without
false claim. I finish quickly, fold the map
to show a thin road headed into broken country.

WITH MY SISTER AT GLACIER BAY

Listen, you said. *Wait for the singing.*
More moan it was than singing, the sound
rising from the ice, it died and began again.

We stood off-shore, the engine idling
as cold leaked across the water from blue-
green walls and ice-fields that stretched
back miles into hunched white ranges.

We carried with us a steady throb and draft
of diesel, brine coated the deck with a dull
glitter. (Remember how salt gritted the dock
where we waited once for the neap tide to cover
the marsh as if that happening would change everything?)

Then a gunshot crack, a blue rift slit
the flat field and slow as a mime's hand
turning, an acre of ice tipped and slid
into still black water. It plunged and rose

a dripping bulk that rolled to one side
and back, sinking, rising, steadying itself
to the draw of its own massive gravity.

Calving, you said. *It's called calving.*
The wake shuddered our boat, we braced
wide against the sway and watched the crag
move to open water. It passed so close

we heard drip and trickle, a rattle of shards
settling, we caught a draft of something raw,
new, dangerous as the smell of birth, of death.

BIKER'S GIRL

Outside Las Brisas Bar & Restaurant, neon
glints on Harleys slanting under the live oaks.
A couple, backlit in the doorway, zip jackets
and step into shadow, the girl's jeans
taut as a black-snake's skin, the seam
studded with stars. She swings behind him
wraps his belly and they wheel onto the highway.

She has painted her fingernails white, on one
scratched a skull to match the blue bruise
needled on his arm. They gather speed in bursts,
slide past condos and cant onto the night beach.
His wrist bends against the throttle, she
leans into the riverbed of his back.

Does the girl know this ride is not whim
but choice? I rode pillion once to show them
I dared, that I was free to choose. We broke fast
from the lot, bent to the curves of a mountain road,
I rejoiced in speed and smell of his sweat, but
returned to safety and a well-mapped road.

Is the girl deafened as I was by wind, danger,
and the unmuffled roar of her body? I gave over
not with trust, but defiance and that was
not enough. I can't tell the girl. If someone
had told me on such a night, I'd have shrugged
and looked to the sky — wild, starry, endless.

THANKS TO CAVAFY

You speak openly of giving over
to lust and the drawn out longing
that follows, even years later
you admonish your body to recall
a particular face, a texture of skin.

I regret I did not know your Alexandria,
the narrow streets, cafes, beaded
doorways, dark V at the neck of rough-
woven kaftans, smells of spice, kif,
men's bodies and the rush of unnamed
wanting, the surrender to pleasure.

Such excesses I never dared but your words
startle recognition — I must know
something of crossing the maelstrom lip,
the slick downward swirl, lessening light
and the hush of judgement silenced.

I thought I had forgotten all that, I meant
to forget, to remember is dangerous as a child's
dream of flying, the easy rise up, the self
alone, separate, holding over earth.

I let go your city of gold light, lovers
I'll never meet, the half-awakened hungers,
but there is time yet to cross to an unknown
place even in this far room where the woodstove
clicks and snow falls outside the window.

WHERE I'VE BEEN

I'm just back, yet where I've been recedes,
edges dim as if I failed to record some
essence of the canyons I passed through, refused
to acknowledge hungers stirred by cedar smoke
or questions that hovered like heat over sageflats
stretching to another dimension of far.

I recall a windmill, a lone adobe house
with blue doorway and strings of red chilis
hung from the vigas — a woman pinned sheets
on the line, the child beside her laughed and ravens
circled as low light raked the mesa.

If I lay claim to that *estancia*, the woman,
the child, if I take them in to memory,
they become mine and with them the old
companion loss also becomes mine.

THE SPACE BETWEEN US

I study old women — there's one who stops
at the bakery for stale bread, another takes
tea at MacDonald's always at the same table.
I look close at their used bodies, the loose

flesh, I want to learn about getting there,
how to cross the space between us and let go
last longings, backward looks, I want
to know about the falling away of old urgencies.

In the next booth, elbows on the table to steady
her hands, she tears open a sugar packet as if
the act was all that mattered, as if she were alone,
performing a miracle in this bright steamy place.

Outside birds gather around the woman
crumbling bread, they nudge close shuffling
small red feet until she flings an arc
and they break in a black burst against the sky.

Does she, intent on her task, not notice
how a sudden cool drops down as slant
shadows ripple across the cobbled square?

APPROACHING THE CRONE

I come into her presence slowly, eyes down
and speak low as to a she-bear, comment
on the long autumn, the asters staying. I
offer no stories, she has heard them all.

I don't look first at her face, but start
with her feet that cling to the ground like toads,
ankles spilling over bone, I let my mind
slide across the rumpled lap, the hidden "V"
beneath the belly's sag, the low-slung breasts.

Hair sprouts from her chin, startling the heart
as did first blood, my eyes meet hers —
clear port-holes opening to a strange sky,
she nods at my wince. I know I am seen.

The tea she offers, an odd dark brew,
reminds me of a place or happening of some importance
not quite remembered and I reach back to a time
before words claimed ownership of form, before
borders closed and fruit was locked in skin.

I trust her silence and the falling away of names,
her gray glance honoring my edgeless uncertainty.

SHE FOLDS HER ARMS

She folds her arms against the wind, alert
to the restless flock shifting down-slope.
Like an old ewe, she has lost envy of new mothers
and watches without stir the ram in rut.

She graced a polished table once, obliged without
taking account but when lust burst like a crowbar
through plaster she pressed her mouth to silence unspeakable
words, then turned to arrange flowers, to order tea.

The children left and hunger for solitude
drew her to the attic's round window. The abandoned
drawing-room lost sheen, silver tarnished,
gold chains coiled unworn in a velvet box.

She watched her husband leave until his car
disappeared behind the hill, then a howl
collected like birth, only this birth pressed
up and her throat let go no sound.

Now wind roils the wheat, clouds pass
fast and on a jagged snag a crow leans
to rasp from the center of its core:
Hear me, hear my voice, this is me.

A BOY BRINGS HIS BLIND GRANDMOTHER A STONE BIRD

He takes from his knapsack the carved stone,
suddenly heavy, too big for the frail nest
of her lap. *An old Eskimo made this.*
She holds out both hands as if to receive
a living thing, as if she knew it needed two hands.

He eases the weight to her knees. Her fingers
round the wing's edge, trail the curve of the tail,
she follows the neck's spiral to where it folds
under a wing and the body accepts itself,
eyes muffled beneath its own feathers.

The boy watches her stroke the rock-grain
that dapples the bird's back, darkens the pinions.
An old Eskimo. She leans over the bird, her breath
riffles the down, her touch rests light as if
the stone-soft breast lifted under her hand.

STAYING IS NOWHERE

(*Denn Bleiben ist nirgends.* Rilke)

I talk of journeys —
trek, voyage, haj —
boast of packing light,
moving out, nights spent
on straw seething with fleas

or beds draped in velvet
and how, crossing the Aegean
I slept on a rope-coil,
the dhow's creak and water's
suck sounding in my dreams.

It isn't travel Rilke meant,
but a break from the mind's
stay, that fastness we claim
as home, the place we look from —
crag, street, chair by the window.

I leave the hills for boulevard
cafes where the crowd passes
at eye level, the air
smells of diesel and linden trees.
When the waiter sets down my glass,

I turn to thank him, he nods
but his eyes give out nothing
and, as it was on the mountain,
loneliness opens to a further
range, another desert.

What is required to move on?
Maps, sextant and compass
fail to indicate a way
from here, but it has happened
when transit cross-hairs

center on a lone pine
aligned with the peak beyond
and I tighten the focus, reckoning
angle, distance, when
hand, eye and what I know

work together, then
for a moment the body forgets
time, place, even purpose
and without effort, without
knowing, I am elsewhere.

ANN B. KNOX grew up in Massachusetts and New York, graduated from Vassar College and lived for fifteen years in Europe and Asia. She now splits her time between a cabin in the Appalachians and Washington, DC. After a decade of teaching elementary school, she received an MFA in writing from Warren Wilson College. For the past twelve years she has edited *Antietam Review* and currently teaches short fiction at the Writer's Center. *Stonecrop*, her first book of poems, was published by the Washington Writers' Publishing House in 1988; *Late Summer Break* (Papier Mache Press), a collection of short stories, appeared in 1995.

Ann Knox's book, *Staying is Nowhere*, is the first in a series of co-published titles with small presses and the Writer's Center, Bethesda, Maryland.